First published in Great Britain in 1993 by
Simon & Schuster Young Books
Campus 400
Maylands Avenue
Hemel Hempstead
Herts HP2 7EZ

Text © 1993 Anne Forsyth
Illustrations © 1993 Thelma Lambert

The right of Anne Forsyth to be identified as the author
of this Work and the right of Thelma Lambert to be
identified as the illustrator of this Work has been
asserted to them in accordance with the Copyright,
Designs and Patents Act 1988.

Typeset in 16pt Bembo by Goodfellow & Egan Ltd, Cambridge
Printed and bound in Portugal by Ediçoes ASA

British Library Cataloguing in Publication Data available

ISBN 0 7500 1239 0
ISBN 0 7500 1240 4 (pbk)

Anne Forsyth

Mandy's Mermaid

Illustrated by Thelma Lambert

SIMON & SCHUSTER
YOUNG BOOKS

Chapter One

"Oh, Mandy," said the teacher. "You haven't been listening." Mandy blinked. She'd been miles away, drifting through an enchanted wood, making up a story about a fairy-tale princess and a magic web.

Mandy sighed and left the enchanted wood. But she soon became really interested in what the teacher was saying.

This term the class was doing a project on the seashore. They would write about the shore, and draw pictures of their finds, and make a collage. Mandy got quite excited. Who knows what we might find, she thought.

Next day the class set out for the shore. The children made their way down the narrow street from school, past the harbour – which was empty today because all the fishing boats were out at sea.

They set off along the sand towards the rocks.

Some children began collecting shells and
seaweed. Some were watching for terns and
oyster catchers and other sea birds. Others
were looking in the rock pools for mussels
and barnacles. Everyone was busy except
Mandy who was dreaming as usual.

She began to scramble over the rocks. "Don't go too far," said the teacher.

Mandy knew that when the tide was out there was a little sandy spot with large rocks. She had almost reached the rocks when she heard a strange sound – a sort of wailing. There was something – or someone – behind the largest rock.

She craned over to see what was making the noise.

To her surprise, it was a girl – a girl with long, straight fair hair. She was sitting on a rock, swaying backwards and forwards and crooning. Mandy moved nearer.

The girl's hair hung down to her waist, and below. Mandy stared. The girl wasn't wearing anything at all, except a long fishy tail.

Mandy gazed. Then she said out loud, "It's a mermaid!" She couldn't believe her luck.

"Oh," said the girl, startled. "You did give me a fright."

"Sorry," Mandy muttered, still staring.

"I thought it would be quiet here," said the mermaid in a whining sort of voice. "But there's hordes of people."

"It's our class," said Mandy. She couldn't stop looking at that long tail all sparkling with fish scales.

"We're doing a project," she added (though in fact Mandy had done very little towards the project).

"Where did you come from?" she asked, becoming a little bolder.

"From the sea, of course," said the mermaid.

"Oh, yes," said Mandy, very humbly.

"If you must know," the mermaid yawned, "I had a row with Mum. I said I was sick of whelks, and she said I was always grumbling and why didn't I clear up my room and . . ."

"Your room?" Mandy gaped.

"Well, my bit of the cave. It's curtained off with seaweed. She went on and on about it being cluttered with shells . . ."

Mandy was rather disappointed. She didn't think mermaids had mothers who made them tidy up their rooms. And mermaids in stories were beautiful. This one certainly had a fishy tail and fair hair but she scowled a lot and had a whiny voice.

Then the teacher, who was keeping a sharp eye on the children to make sure that no one wandered off or got into trouble, called, "Mandy!"

"Wait there," said Mandy to the mermaid, and she went scrambling back over the rocks.

By this time the other children had found shells and seaweed and interesting sea creatures. They would take the shells and seaweed, but not living things, back to the classroom.

"I've got some shells, all different," said Emily.

"I found a star fish," said Paul. Some had found limpets and barnacles and razor shells. Others had found different kinds of seaweed.

"I found a mermaid," said Mandy.

"Oh, Mandy, really!" said the teacher.

"Honestly," said Mandy. "Just behind that rock. Come on, look!"

The teacher smiled. "All right then." She followed Mandy and so did the other children.

"Listen!" said Mandy. "You can hear her
singing. She's just behind that big rock."

And with that, there was a splash. They
couldn't see anything but a ripple on the
water.

"Oh, Mandy," said the teacher. "You do
make up stories. It was just a fish. Come
on, everyone, time we went back."

Mandy was very cross. All right, she
made up stories, but this one was true.

Chapter Two

Next day was Saturday. After lunch, Mum said, "The dog needs a good walk and I can't take him today." Topper, the dog, sat with his head on one side.

"All right," said Sara, Mandy's big sister. "I'll take him on the shore. Coming, Mandy?"

Mandy and her family – Mum, Dad, and Sara (and Topper) – lived in an old stone house overlooking the shore. Mandy liked to look out over the waves. "Just imagine," she thought, "maybe there's a palace under the sea. And they have great feasts served by dolphins on cockleshells."

"Really, Mandy," Mum sometimes said a little crossly, "you're always day-dreaming."

That Saturday afternoon, Mandy and
Sara set off for the shore, with Topper on
his lead. Topper liked splashing in the sea
and chasing sticks, so Sara took off his lead
and they were soon racing across the sands.
Mandy followed slowly.

Then she heard the singing. She
scrambled over the rocks, and there was the
mermaid, combing her hair and humming
tunelessly.

"You shouldn't have gone off like that," said Mandy. "No one believed me."

"Hard luck," said the mermaid. "I went home," she added. "I didn't want to miss my tea." She said pathetically, "I don't suppose you've got anything to eat, have you?"

Mandy felt in her pocket. "I've got a packet of crisps. Prawn flavour."

"Mmm . . ." The mermaid ripped open he packet and began crunching. 'Yummy . . ."

"What's it like under the sea?" Mandy vas longing to know.

The mermaid yawned. "Nothing but caves and seaweed and no one to talk to. Fish are the dullest creatures – and they're scared of us mermaids anyway. There are seals sometimes – and dolphins, but they're boring too."

"But what about parties and feasts? I thought there might be a sea palace," said Mandy a little desperately. She was beginning to be disappointed in the mermaid.

"Well, the Bass Rock mermaids are giving a party next week – but they're such a snooty lot. I wish I had a new brush and comb, and looked – well, different," said the mermaid.

"My sister has a special brush," said Mandy. "She wouldn't mind if you borrowed it."

The mermaid brightened up.

"And – er – what do you call it? Make-up?" said the mermaid. "I've seen people on the sands wearing paint on their faces and red on their lips."

"Lipstick," said Mandy. "I'll see what I can find."

"Great," said the mermaid, not adding "thank you". She seemed rather rude, thought Mandy, but then you couldn't expect mermaids to be like ordinary people.

"Another thing," said Mandy, "why do you always sing that wailing song, if you don't mind me asking?"

"It's the only one I know," said the mermaid, sulking again.

"I know lots of good songs," said Mandy. "Pop songs. I'll teach you another, if you like."

"Don't mind," said the mermaid.

"There's a mermaid on the rocks," said
Mandy, when she caught up with Sara.
"With a long fishy tail," she added. "She'd
like to borrow your styling brush and
make-up."

"You do talk a lot of rubbish," said Sara.
"Come on, Topper, time to go home."

Chapter Three

"Well, I *did* ask," said Mandy next day as she borrowed Sara's brush and make-up, and popped them into a bag.

When next Mandy and Mum went out with the dog, Mandy climbed over the rocks. The mermaid was there, waiting. Mandy brought the bag out of her pocket.

"Mmm . . ." said the mermaid, as she opened it. "What's this?"

"Blusher," said Mandy crossly. "You put it on your cheeks to give you colour." The mermaid didn't seem at all grateful. And Sara would probably be very annoyed when she found some of her make-up had vanished.

A few days later, Mandy hardly knew the mermaid. Her straight fringe was curled and she had made up her face.

But she still complained. "After the Bass Rock party, there won't be any other parties for ages. Life's so dull."

Mandy was beginning to be sorry she
had been kind to this bad-tempered
creature. Then she had an idea.

"You could come to the Gala."

"What's that?" The mermaid yawned
again.

"It's every year," said Mandy. "It's for
the schools – well, for everyone, really.
There's a procession and we decorate the
lorries. Our school's doing a lorry about
the seashore with sand and fishing
nets . . . ." Her voice trailed off.

Suddenly she had had a brainwave.

"You could be on our lorry! It's called a
float, actually," she explained.

"No," said the mermaid.

"Please!" said Mandy. "We all dress up. It'll be fun."

"No way," said the mermaid and dived beneath the waves.

Mandy followed Mum and Topper home, very cross indeed. "I'm finished with her," she said.

But a few days later, gathering shells with Sara, she heard a strange sound – like someone singing.

She knew right away it was one of the pop songs she had taught the mermaid.

"Hello," said the mermaid, as Mandy climbed over the rocks. "I've thought about it. I'll be on your float. But I don't want people laughing at me because I'm a mermaid. I want to look beautiful. I want to dress up."

Mandy had never heard anyone say "I want" quite so often. She sighed. "OK. I'll see what I can do."

On the way home Mandy thought about it. Then she knew exactly what she needed. It was in the dressing-up box at school, and it hadn't been used since the pantomime last Christmas. She was sure the teacher wouldn't mind.

"What do you want it for?" asked the teacher.

"It's for a friend to wear in the Gala," said Mandy.

"Well, come along and we'll see if it's still there." She delved into the box, and there it was, wrapped in tissue paper.

"Oh, thank you," Mandy beamed. "I'll take great care of it."

That day Mandy could hardly wait to see the mermaid. Surely this would make her smile.

"I've brought you something to wear in the procession," said Mandy.

"Wow!" said the mermaid, and her face broke into a smile. "Diamonds!"

"Well," said Mandy, "Not real diamonds. But it's a tiara."

The mermaid tried it on, and admired her reflection in a pool. "Mmm . . ." she said. "I don't mind being in your procession."

Actually, Mandy knew that the mermaid
was longing to be in the procession,
especially now that she had the tiara to
wear. Because there was nothing the
mermaid enjoyed quite as much as showing
off.

"Right," said Mandy. "But I wonder
how I can get you on to the float. The floats
will be parked on the front, near the
harbour. Could you manage to get on to
the quay? I'll help you."

"I'll manage," said the mermaid. "But I
can't be out of the water too long. You'll
need buckets of water, so that I don't get
too dry."

"I'll do what I can," promised Mandy.

"Come on, Mandy," called Mum. "What *are* you doing?"

At home, Mandy found two plastic buckets. She would fill them at the tap down by the harbour. If she kept refilling the buckets – and surely her friend Lisa would help – they could keep the mermaid wet. It wasn't far from the harbour up to the Town Hall where the procession ended.

She was quite proud of herself for thinking of this. "Use your common sense," Mum kept saying. Well, this time she had.

Chapter Four

Mandy's class had gone to a lot of trouble
to decorate the float. They had a lobster
creel and fishing nets, and buckets of shells,
and seaweed. One girl was a fishwife, in a
striped skirt and shawl. Some boys were
fishermen, pretending to draw in the nets.
Mandy was to be in the middle, pretending
to build a sandcastle.

When Mandy arrived at half-past one, with her buckets, there were lots of people around. "Listen," she said to Lisa, "would you help . . .?" And then to her astonishment, she saw the mermaid already on the float. She was sitting on a fish box and she was wearing the tiara, slightly askew. She had curled her fringe and was wearing make-up.

"I got here on my own," she said. "But I'm so cold." Mandy did hope she wasn't going to sulk.

"Look," she said, "have my anorak."
"Who on earth's that?" said Mandy's
acher.

"A friend of mine," said Mandy. "She's a –" she nearly said "a mermaid", then changed it to "dressed up as a mermaid."

"Who's that?" asked another teacher.

"A friend of Mandy's."

"Must be from the Secondary."

"Well, I suppose it's all right. She's gone to such trouble with her costume. Really splendid."

"Look," said a very young child. "A fish."

"Don't be silly," said his big sister. "It's a mermaid, but not a real one. You never saw a mermaid wearing an anorak. It's just someone dressed up."

The parade moved off, led by the Gala Queen and her attendants in a vintage car.

The mermaid took off her anorak and began combing her hair.

And then it began to rain, a few drops at first, then it became a steady drizzle. People put up umbrellas and huddled under plastic capes. But the mermaid was delighted. She was all wet, just as wet as if she'd been in the sea. Mandy was pleased too – now there was no need to run backwards and forwards with buckets of water. And the mermaid was smiling!

All the way until the procession stopped in front of the town hall, she waved and smiled.

"Isn't she great! What a good costume!" people said.

When the judges reached Mandy's float, they immediately handed a first-prize ticket to the teacher in charge. Second were the pirates from another school who had been singing "Yo, ho, ho" all the way and were quite hoarse by now.

Chapter five

After all that, the children got down from
the floats and went off to see the old fire
engines or watch the Highland dancers.
The mermaid sat on the lorry, still smiling.
And it rained and rained.

From time to time, Mandy came back to
bring her a packet of crisps or a choc ice.
Soon the mermaid had chocolate all round
her mouth and her tiara had slipped.

Half way through the afternoon, the children queued up for bags of food – each one got a paper bag with a bun and a cake and a biscuit, and a carton of juice.

"Can I have two bags, please?" asked Mandy.

"Sorry, only one each," said the teacher who was giving them out.

"It's for my friend."

"Tell her to come along herself."

The teacher turned to another member of the staff. "You do have to watch. There's always someone tries to get two bags . . ."

So Mandy went back to the mermaid and
they shared the bag of food and the carton
of juice.

Then Mandy went off to watch the tug of
war. A little later, she thought she'd better
see how the mermaid was getting on. It was
still raining, but she would probably be
happier back in the sea. But to Mandy's
horror, the floats had gone.

"Where's our lorry?" Mandy asked a boy
who was sucking an ice lolly nearby.

"Gone back to the harbour."

"Come on!" said Mandy to Lisa. "I must find out what's happened to her."

"Happened to who?" said Lisa, rather puzzled.

"The mermaid, of course," said Mandy.

"But I thought . . ." said Lisa. Surely it hadn't been a *real* mermaid?

"Come *on*!" said Mandy.

They ran all the way from the town park down to the harbour. There was the lorry with its fishing nets and buckets and shells. The drivers had left the floats and gone off for a cup of tea.

And there on the box where the mermaid had sat, was the tiara.

Later, the children were helping to clear the float.

"The mermaid looked splendid," said the teacher. "What happened to your friend, Mandy? And who was she?"

"Er . . ." said Mandy, because she didn't really know what had happened.

Mandy never saw the mermaid again. But deep down under the sea, the mermaid was telling everyone about her adventures.

She made a special trip to tell the Bass Rock mermaids.

In time, the sea creatures became rather tired of hearing the story.

"I bet she made it all up," said one.

"Fancy being in a parade," said another.

"Well, I don't believe a word of it," said a passing seal. "A fishy tale, if you ask me."

But the mermaid just smiled.

Mandy thought about the mermaid
sometimes. And one summer evening,
when it was light long after bedtime, the
family went for a walk along the shore.

Suddenly, over the waves, you could
hear a voice singing a pop song.

"People with radios," said Mum,
"shouldn't be allowed."

"Tuneless rubbish," said Dad, who liked
Scottish fiddle music.

"I can sing better than that," said Sara.

Topper raised his head and howled.

But Mandy didn't say anything. She
knew just who was singing.